This paperback edition first published in 2016 by Andersen Press Ltd.
First published in Great Britain in 2015 by Andersen Press Ltd.,
20 Vauxhall Bridge Road, London SW1V 2SA.
Colour separated in Switzerland by Photolitho AG, Zürich.
Printed and bound in China.

1 3 5 7 9 10 8 6 4 2

British Library Cataloguing in Publication Data available.
ISBN 9781783442065

www.richardbyrne.co.uk

Other books by Richard Byrne:
PENGUINS CAN'T FLY!

For Max, David, Martin, Teresa,
Charlotte and Christopher.

Richard Byrne

Spotty Lottie and Me

Andersen Press

Joey had chicken pox and had to stay at home.
He was really missing his friends.

"Being ill is **boring!**" he complained.
"You can play with a friend," said Joey's mummy,
"but they will have to be a spotty one, because
you are still **infectious.**"

Joey thought about where he might
find a spotty friend.

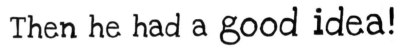

Then he had a **good idea!**

"Hello, spotty leopard, will **you** play with me?" he asked.

Leopard took **one** look at Joey and explained that he **had** to be Somewhere else.

Joey didn't
have much luck
elsewhere.

Snake said he was terribly sorry,
but he was late for an appointment
and had to skedaddle...

...Cheetah had to dash...

...nor did dalmatian, peacock, gecko or frog.

...and giraffe didn't
hang around
for long...

Even ladybird said

she had to fly.

Soon after
Joey returned home,
there was a **knock**
at the **door**.

It was...

Joey and Lottie had a **lot** of **fun** together and after a few days...

...their **spots**
began to disappear.

Now that Joey's spots had gone, all the animals wanted to play too.

But as they came **nearer...**

"Now what's **wrong**?" asked Joey.